Charlie

THE

Choo-Choo

by

Beryl Evans

with illustrations based on original artwork by Ned Dameron

Copyright © 1942

Fourth Edition

SIMON & SCHUSTER BOOKS FOR YOUNG READERS

New York London Toronto Sydney New Delhi

Bob Brooks was an engineer for the Mid-World Railway Company, on the St. Louis to Topeka run. Engineer Bob was the best trainman the Mid-World Railway Company ever had, and Charlie was the best train!

Charlie was a 402 Big Boy steam locomotive, and Engineer Bob was the only man who had ever been allowed to sit in his peek-seat and pull the whistle.

Everyone knew the *WHOOO-OOOO* of Charlie's whistle, and whenever they heard it echoing across the flat Kansas countryside, they said, "There goes Charlie and Engineer Bob, the fastest team between St. Louis and Topeka!" Boys and girls ran into their yards to watch Charlie and Engineer Bob go by. Engineer Bob would smile and wave. The children would smile and wave back.

Engineer Bob had a special secret. He was the only one who knew. Charlie the Choo-Choo was really, really alive.

One day while they were making the run between Topeka and St. Louis, Engineer Bob heard singing, very soft and low.

"Who is in the cab with me?" Engineer Bob said sternly.

"Don't worry," said a small, gruff voice. "It is only I."

"Who's I?" Engineer Bob asked. He spoke in his biggest, sternest voice, because he thought someone was playing a joke on him.

"Charlie," said the small, gruff voice.

"Hardy har-har!" said Engineer Bob. "Trains can't talk! I may not know much, but I know that! If you're Charlie, I suppose you can blow your own whistle!"

"Of course," said the small, gruff voice, and just then the whistle made its big noise, rolling out across the Missouri plains: *WHOOO-OOOO!*

"Goodness!" said Engineer Bob. "It really is you!"

"I told you," said Charlie the Choo-Choo.

"How come I never knew you were alive before?" asked Engineer Bob. "Why didn't you ever talk to me before?"

Then Charlie sang this song to Engineer Bob in his small, gruff voice:

Don't ask me silly questions, I won't play silly games.
I'm just a simple choo-choo train, and I'll always be the same.
I only want to race along, beneath the bright blue sky,
and be a happy choo-choo train, until the day I die.

"Will you talk to me some more when we're making our run?" asked Engineer Bob. "I'd like that."

"I would, too," said Charlie. "I love you, Engineer Bob."

"I love you too, Charlie," said Engineer Bob, and then he blew the whistle himself, just to show how happy he was. *WHOOO-OOO!* It was the biggest and best Charlie had ever whistled, and everyone who heard it came out to see.

Engineer Bob and Charlie spent many happy days together and talked of many things. Engineer Bob lived alone, and Charlie was the first real friend he'd had since his wife died, long ago, in New York.

One day, when Charlie and Engineer Bob returned to the roundhouse in St. Louis, they found a new diesel locomotive in Charlie's berth. And what a diesel locomotive it was! Five thousand horsepower! Stainless steel couplers! Traction motors from the Utica Engine Works in Utica, New York! And sitting on top, behind the generator, were three bright-yellow radiator cooling fans.

"What is this?" Engineer Bob asked in a worried voice, but Charlie only sang his song in his smallest, gruffest voice:

Don't ask me silly questions, I won't play silly games.
I'm just a simple choo-choo train, and I'll always be the same.
I only want to race along, beneath the bright blue sky,
and be a happy choo-choo train, until the day I die.

Mr. Briggs, the roundhouse manager, came over.

"That is a beautiful diesel locomotive," said Engineer Bob, "but you will have to move it out of Charlie's berth, Mr. Briggs. Charlie needs a lube job this very afternoon."

"Charlie won't be needing any more lube jobs, Engineer Bob," said Mr. Briggs sadly. "This is his replacement—a brand-new Burlington Zephyr diesel loco. Once, Charlie was the best locomotive in the world, but now he is old and his boiler leaks. I am afraid the time has come for Charlie to retire."

"Nonsense!" Engineer Bob was mad! "Charlie is still full of zip and zowie! I will telegraph the head office of the Mid-World Railway Company! I will telegraph the president, Mr. Raymond Martin, myself! I know him because he once gave me a Good Service Award, and afterwards Charlie and I took his little daughter for a ride. I let her pull the lanyard, and Charlie whistled his loudest for her!"

"I am sorry, Bob," said Mr. Briggs. "It was Mr. Martin himself who ordered the new diesel loco."

It was true. And so Charlie the Choo-Choo was shunted off to a siding in the farthest corner of Mid-World's St. Louis yard to rust in the weeds.

Now the *HONNNK! HONNNK!* of the Burlington Zephyr was heard on the St. Louis to Topeka run, and Charlie's whistle blew no more.

A family of mice nested in the seat where Engineer Bob once sat so proudly, watching the countryside speed past; a family of swallows nested in his smokestack.

Charlie was lonely and very sad. He missed the steel tracks and bright blue skies and wide open spaces. Sometimes, late at night, he thought of these things and cried dark, oily tears. This rusted his fine Stratham headlight, but he didn't care, because now the Stratham headlight was old, and it was always dark.

Mr. Martin, the president of the Mid-World Railway Company, wrote and offered to put Engineer Bob in the peek-seat of the new Burlington Zephyr.

"It is a fine loco, Engineer Bob," said Mr. Martin, "chock-full of zip and zowie, and you should be the one to pilot it! Of all the engineers who work for Mid-World, you are the best. And my daughter Susannah has never forgotten that you let her pull old Charlie's whistle."

But Engineer Bob said that if he couldn't pilot Charlie, his days as a trainman were done. "I wouldn't understand such a fine new diesel loco," said Engineer Bob, "and it wouldn't understand me." He was given a job cleaning the engines in the St. Louis yards, and Engineer Bob became Wiper Bob.

The other engineers who drove the fine new diesels would laugh at him. "Look at that old fool!" they'd say. "He cannot understand that the world has moved on!"

Sometimes, late at night, Engineer Bob would go to the far side of the rail yard, where Charlie the Choo-Choo stood on the rusty rails of the lonely siding that had become his home. Weeds had twined in his wheels; his headlight was rusty and dark. Engineer Bob always talked to Charlie, but Charlie replied less and less. Many nights Charlie would not talk at all.

One night, a terrible idea came into Engineer Bob's head. "Charlie, are you dying?" he asked.

In his smallest, gruffest voice, Charlie replied:

Don't ask me silly questions, I won't play silly games.
I'm just a simple choo-choo train, and I'll always be the same.
Now that I can't race along, beneath the bright blue sky,
I guess that I'll just sit right here, until I finally die.

Mr. Martin, the president of the Mid-World Railway Company, came to St. Louis to check on the operation. His plan was to ride the Burlington Zephyr to Topeka, where his daughter was giving her first piano recital, that very afternoon. Only the Zephyr wouldn't start. There was water in the diesel fuel, it seemed. All the other trains were out on their runs! What to do?

Someone tugged Mr. Martin's arm. It was Wiper Bob, only he no longer looked like an engine wiper. He had taken off his oil-stained dungarees and put on a clean pair of overalls. On his head was his old pillow-tick engineer's cap.

"Charlie is right over there, on that siding," he said. "Charlie will make the run to Topeka, Mr. Martin. Charlie will get you there in time for your daughter's piano recital."

"That old steamer?" scoffed Mr. Briggs. "Charlie would still be fifty miles out of Topeka at sundown!"

"Charlie can do it," Engineer Bob insisted. "Without a train to pull, I know he can! I have been cleaning his engine and his boiler in my spare time, you see."

"We'll give it a try," said Mr. Martin. "I would be sorry to miss Susannah's first recital!"

Charlie was all ready to go; Engineer Bob had filled his tender with fresh coal, and the firebox was so hot its sides were red. He helped Mr. Martin up into the cab and backed Charlie off the rusty, forgotten siding and onto the main track for the first time in years. Then, as he engaged Forward First, he pulled on the lanyard and Charlie gave his old brave cry: *WHOOO-OOOOO!*

All over St. Louis the children heard that cry, and ran out into their yards to watch the rusty old steam loco pass.

"Look!" they cried. "It's Charlie! Charlie the Choo-Choo is back! Hurrah!" They all waved, and as Charlie steamed out of town, gathering speed, he blew his own whistle, just as he had in the old days: *WHOOOO-OOOOOOO!*

Clickety-clack went Charlie's wheels! *Chuffa-chuffa* went the smoke from Charlie's stack! *Brump-brump* went the conveyor as it fed coal into the firebox! Talk about zip! Talk about zowie! Golly gee, gosh, and wowie! Charlie had never gone so fast before! The countryside went whizzing by in a blur! They passed the cars on Route 41 as if they were standing still!

"Hoptedoodle!" cried Mr. Martin, waving his hat in the air. "This is some locomotive, Bob! I don't know why we ever retired it! How do you keep the coal conveyor loaded at this speed?"

Engineer Bob only smiled, because he knew Charlie was feeding himself. And, beneath the *clickety-clack* and the *chuffa-chuffa* and the *brump-brump*, he could hear Charlie singing his old song in his low, gruff voice:

Don't ask me silly questions, I won't play silly games.
I'm just a simple choo-choo train, and I'll always be the same.
I only want to race along, beneath the bright blue sky,
and be a happy choo-choo train, until the day I die.

Charlie got Mr. Martin to his daughter's piano recital on time (of course), and Susannah was just tickled pink to see her old friend Charlie again (of course), and they all went back to St. Louis together with Susannah yanking hell out of the train whistle the whole way.

Mr. Martin got Charlie and Engineer Bob a gig pulling kids around the brand-new Mid-World Amusement Park and Fun Fair in California, and you will find them there to this day, pulling laughing children hither and thither in that world of lights and music and good, wholesome fun.

Engineer Bob's hair is white, and Charlie doesn't talk as much as he once did, but both of them still have plenty of zip and zowie.

And every now and then the children hear Charlie singing his old song in his soft, gruff voice.

THE END

SIMON & SCHUSTER BOOKS FOR YOUNG READERS

An imprint of Simon & Schuster Children's Publishing Division

1230 Avenue of the Americas, New York, New York 10020

Text copyright © 2016 by Beryl Evans

Cover illustrations copyright © 2016 by Ned Dameron

Interior illustrations copyright © 2016 by Columbia TriStar Marketing Group, Inc.

All rights reserved, including the right of reproduction in whole or in part in any form.

SIMON & SCHUSTER BOOKS FOR YOUNG READERS is a trademark of Simon & Schuster, Inc.

For information about special discounts for bulk purchases, please contact

Simon & Schuster Special Sales at 1-866-506-1949 or business@simonandschuster.com.

The Simon & Schuster Speakers Bureau can bring authors to your live event.

For more information or to book an event, contact the Simon & Schuster Speakers Bureau

at 1-866-248-3049 or visit our website at www.simonspeakers.com.

The text for this book was set in Adobe Garamond.

Manufactured in the United States of America

1016 LAK

First Simon & Schuster Books for Young Readers hardcover edition November 2016

2 4 6 8 10 9 7 5 3 1

CIP data for this book is available from the Library of Congress.

ISBN 978-1-5344-0123-5

ISBN 978-1-5344-0124-2 (eBook)